Produced by Kroha Associates, Inc.
Middletown, Connecticut

Illustrated by Yakovetic Productions

Written by M.C. Varley

Printed in the United States of America.

ISBN 1-56326-173-1

Ariel's Painting Party

One morning the Little Mermaid awoke very early and swam to the lagoon just in time to see the sun beginning to rise over the island. The soft yellow rays of light bathed the island in a warm, wonderful glow. *What a lovely picture this would make,* Ariel thought. *And I'm just the person to paint it!*

She raced to her grotto to fetch her paints, then quickly swam back to the lagoon and started painting.

A little while later Scuttle the seagull flew by and asked Ariel what she was doing. "I'm painting a picture of this lovely sunrise," she told him. "That way I'll always have something to remind me of how beautiful it is."

"It's a nice picture," Scuttle said, "but I think it needs more birds."

"No, no, no, that's not what it needs," said Sebastian the crab, who was wandering by on his morning walk. "What it needs is more crabs — and, of course, a nice garden growing right over there."

Just then Flounder the fish and his sister Sandy arrived. "It's a very pretty picture, Ariel," said Sandy. "But shouldn't there be more fish in it?"

"More fish?" squawked Scuttle. "It needs more birds!"

"And I say there are already too many birds," replied Sebastian. "What it needs is more crabs!"

Soon Scales the dragon dropped by to see what all the commotion was about.

"Oh, Scales," cried Ariel. "All I wanted to do was paint a picture of this beautiful day, but everyone keeps interrupting me, trying to get me to paint their way!"

"Maybe we should all paint pictures, just the way we want to," Scales suggested. "And then we can have an exhibit of everybody's paintings."

"That's a wonderful idea!" Ariel said. "And we can let my father, King Triton, decide which one is the best!"

Ariel told the others about Scales's plan. Everyone thought it was a terrific idea. "But we'll need more paint," Sebastian pointed out.

"And more brushes, too," added Scuttle.

"And don't forget more paper!" said Sandy.

Ariel swam back to her grotto to get more paint while Scales and Sebastian collected huge palm leaves for each of them to use as paper. And Scuttle supplied some old tail feathers that had fallen out in his nest to help make the paintbrushes.

Soon everyone was busily painting away. Ariel continued painting the sun as it rose over the island, while…

Scuttle painted a sky filled with birds winging their way over the treetops.

Sebastian painted a scene of a picnic at his tidal pool garden. Every crab from miles around was there!

Scales painted his comfortable cave, surrounded by tall trees and fresh flowers and the clean, clear, murmuring waters of the lagoon.

Flounder and Sandy painted pictures of themselves playing in the water. While Flounder frolicked with a whale and an octopus in his painting, Sandy swam with the frisky seahorses in hers.

When he was through painting his own picture, Scuttle peeked over Sebastian's shoulder to see how the crab was doing. Then he slid around behind Scales's tail to look at the dragon's picture, too.

"Ha!" squawked Scuttle when he'd seen what they had done. "I'm going to win the contest for sure! Your paintings don't look anything like the island!"

"You don't know what you're talking about!" shouted Sebastian. "My picture is clearly the winning picture. It's much better than yours."

"No, ours are the best," Flounder and Sandy called out. "Anyone can see that."

"But you didn't paint the island at all," replied Scales. "You just painted the water around it. My painting is the only one that is truly a picture of the island."

"Here comes my father," said Ariel. "He'll know which one is really the best."

They all crowded around the king, eager for him to choose the winning picture. "These paintings are all very nice," the king said, placing them carefully on the easels. "But none of them is the best by itself."

"I don't understand," cried Ariel. "You promised you'd tell us which was the best!"

"Let me show you," replied the king.

Then King Triton took all the paintings and rearranged them. When he finished, the friends saw what the king meant.

"You see," said the king, "our island is an amazing place. No one picture by itself can capture all its beauty and charm. But when you look at the island from everyone's point of view, you get a picture that is truly the best."

"You're right!" exclaimed Ariel. "Our island makes a beautiful picture — and we're *all* just the ones to paint it!"